To my darling daughter, Francesca, on your very first Christmas. I wish you many happy hours of reading and looking at pictures. Hugs and kisses.
Love,
Mamma

BABAR'S
ANNIVERSARY
ALBUM

 RANDOM HOUSE

BABAR'S
ANNIVERSARY ALBUM

6 FAVORITE STORIES

by

JEAN and LAURENT DE BRUNHOFF

Introduction
by
MAURICE SENDAK

NEW YORK

CONTENTS

The stories in this volume are abridged. The three stories by Jean de Brunhoff are based on the translation from the French by Merle S. Haas.

Copyright © 1981 by Random House, Inc. Introduction © 1981 by Maurice Sendak. Babar the King © 1935, renewed 1963 by Random House, Inc. The Story of Babar © 1933, renewed 1961 by Random House, Inc. The Travels of Babar © 1934, renewed 1962 by Random House, Inc. Babar's Birthday Surprise © 1970 by Laurent de Brunhoff. Babar and the Wully-Wully © 1975 by Laurent de Brunhoff. Babar's Mystery © 1978 by Laurent de Brunhoff. All rights reserved under International and Pan-American Copyright Conventions. Published in the United States by Random House, Inc., New York, and simultaneously in Canada by Random House of Canada Limited, Toronto. Library of Congress Cataloging in Publication Data: Brunhoff, Jean de, 1899–1937. Babar's anniversary album. Contents: The story of Babar —The travels of Babar —Babar the king —Babar's mystery —[etc.] 1. Children's stories, French —Translations into English. 2. Children's stories, English —Translations from French. [1. Elephants —Fiction] I. Brunhoff, Laurent de, 1925– . II. Title. PZ7.B793Bab 1981 843'.914'08036 [Fic] 81-5182 AACR2 ISBN: 0-394-84813-6 (trade); 0-394-94813-0 (lib. bdg.)
Manufactured in the United States of America   5 6 7 8 9 0

Maman Éléphant et Bibi Éléphant
se promènent
dans la forêt
Très heureux

Mais
le vilain chasseur tire
et tue Maman Éléphant
Bibi Éléphant pleure.—

Homage to Babar
on His 50th Birthday

BY MAURICE SENDAK

Picture Story

BY LAURENT DE BRUNHOFF

Babar's escape to Paris, when he fled the jungle in 1931, was not, alas, via Brooklyn. If he had come my way, how I would have welcomed that little orphaned elephant and smothered him with affection. What a pity he didn't visit my house; some of that gentle spirit, those sensible ways, might have rubbed off on a child whose childhood was largely governed by ungoverned emotions. When I did make his acquaintance, as a young artist in the early 1950s, it was too late. By then, raised on a diet of Sturm und Drang, I inwardly condemned the Babar books for what I considered an overly reasoned approach to life: typically French, I said then. About this last judgment I was right, but not in my negative inference. So although I admired the whole series of books, their Gallic tone, which I interpreted as aloofness, continued to rankle. And while I loved the Babars, I loved them purely for their graphic splendor.

After all, the French, at the turn of the century, had practically reinvented the illustrated book. Along with the work of André Hellé, Edy Legrand, Boutet de Monvel, Felix Vallotton, and Pierre Bonnard, de Brunhoff shared a freedom and charm, a freshness of vision that captivates and takes the breath away. Like an extravagant piece of poetry, the interplay between few words and many pictures, commonly called the picture book, is a difficult, exquisite, and most easily collapsible form that few have mastered. The successful results are so ingenious and profound that they should rightfully take their place with comparably sophisticated "grown-up" works of art.

Jean de Brunhoff was a master of this form. Between 1931 and 1937 he completed a body of work that forever changed the face of the illustrated book. Undoubtedly he had no such ambition. Like

The drawing on the facing page was one of many early sketches my father made of the sensitive scene from *The Story of Babar* in which Babar's mother is killed by a hunter. The action shown here, all on one page, was ultimately broken into two separate pages.

William Nicholson, who created two of England's best picture books, *Clever Bill* and *The Pirate Twins*, to amuse his children, de Brunhoff, inspired by his wife and young sons, created Babar.

Jean de Brunhoff was born in 1899. His father, Maurice, a Frenchman of Baltic and Swedish origins, was a publisher of art magazines, among them the very beautiful *Program of Serge Diaghilev's Ballets Russes*. Jean, in fact, came from a family of publishers; his brother Michel was editor-in-chief of the French *Vogue* and his brother-in-law Lucien Vogel published the fashion magazine *Le Jardin des Modes* and later *Vu*. Jean was a painter who put himself somewhere on the edge of the avant-garde stream. In 1924 he married Cecile Sabouraud, a pianist, and it is forever to her credit that one day in 1931 she invented the story of a little elephant to amuse the two young de Brunhoff children, Mathieu and Laurent. The children enthusiastically related the story to their papa, and thus began Babar.

My early indifference to de Brunhoff's writing was, in retrospect, a curious and significant blind spot. I was busy then, furiously learning what a picture book was and, more to the point, what it could be. That learning consisted mostly of swooping, magpie-like, into the works of Randolph Caldecott, Beatrix Potter, William Nicholson, and Edward Ardizzone and taking away what most suited my creative purposes. This was in the 1950s. I was then a green recruit fresh from the analyst's couch and woe betide the work that failed to loudly signal its Freudian allegiance. With a convert's proverbial fervor I rushed pell-mell into the very heart of what I considered Babar's unresolved problem: his mother's death, of course.

I never quite got over that death. It was a landmark experience for me in children's literature. The ease and remarkable calm with which de Brunhoff blighted the life of his baby elephant numbed me. That sublimely happy babyhood lost, after only two full pages, and then, as in a nightmare (and too much like life), Babar, cruelly and arbitrarily deprived of his loving mother, runs wildly out of babyhood (the innocent jungle) and into cozy, amnesia-inducing society (Paris, only blocks away from that jungle). It is there that he feverishly embraces adulthood, culture, manners, any surface, to hide the hideous trauma of that useless death. Or so it seemed to me then. Why, I wondered, give us a mother's death and then deprive us of a fulsome wallowing in its gory psychological repercussions? Why not, in fact, go back and find another less volatile reason for Babar to flee the jungle? Easy enough solution, thought I. In summation, I judged this death to be a gratuitously punishing touch, an issue raised and bewilderingly passed over. Simply, I missed the point. It took years of further exposure to the work of many different artists, my own redefinition of the picture book form, and much growing up to complete my appreciation of Babar. Now, from a distance of more

This picture of Jean de Brunhoff was taken in September 1930 at the very time he was creating Babar. The photo was taken in the garden at Chessy, his father-in-law's country home east of Paris, where we always spent our summers. My father was already an accomplished painter before he began the Babar stories. The painting of Chessy, shown on the facing page, was made by him in 1927 and is representative of his painting style.

Chessy, where Babar was born.

My mother, my brother Mathieu in the center, and me in 1931.

Mathieu and me with our little brother, Thierry, and our beloved dog, Truffle, in 1936. Truffle was the inspiration for the little spotted dog that played a big part in my father's last book, *Babar and Father Christmas*.

Here is another painting my father made in 1927, showing me at age two on my rocking horse. Perhaps it was this rocking horse that gave my father the idea of having Babar ride a wooden horse in the grand parade in *Babar the King*. What is not speculation is how the first idea of Babar came to my father. One day in 1930 my mother told Mathieu and me a story about a little elephant. We enjoyed it so much that we repeated it to our father, who developed the plot to make a book for us. Why he named the little elephant Babar no one knows.

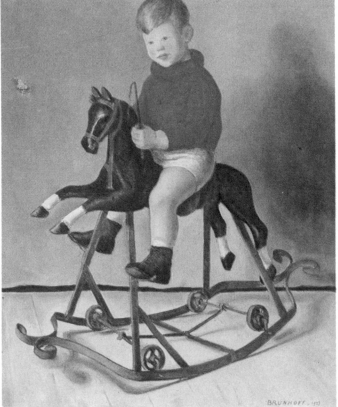

My father so enjoyed his new craft of storytelling and illustrating that he began work on his second book before *The Story of Babar* was published in 1931. *The Travels of Babar* was published in 1932 and his third book, *Babar the King,* in 1933. Later came *Babar and His Children,* inspired by our family, though ours was a family of three boys while Babar's was two boys and a girl.

Photo Schall

This photo of my father was taken in 1936. By then he was well known for his Babar stories.

Here are the first sketches of Babar standing up and wearing his green suit and bowler hat, and the first sketch of Babar's and the Old Lady's famous good-bye kiss in *The Story of Babar*. Though my father created the Old Lady to play the role of an indulgent granny, he gave her a slim, youthful figure remarkably like my mother's.

10

than thirty years, Babar is at the very heart of my conception of what turns a picture book into a work of art. The graphics are tightly linked to the deceptively loose prose-poetry style that is astonishing in its ease of expression. The pictures, rather than merely echoing the text, enrich and expand Babar's world.

Laurent de Brunhoff, Jean's eldest son, and I are colleagues and old, good friends. In large part it is Laurent who urged me out of my frantic Freudian "dig," without ever denying the existence of those significant clues in Jean's Babar. He helped adjust my extremist view of his father's work to a more moderated, clear-cut understanding.

In the summer of 1977 Laurent invited me to his family home. We took the train at Gare St. Lazare to the small village of Epône and then walked a memorable two miles through the Seine valley to his house. It is an old, rather plain, stone villa surrounded by a high wall and covered with ivy. Marie-Claude and Anne, Laurent's wife and daughter, were there to greet me. In the garden I met Mme. Jean de Brunhoff, a beautiful, wonderfully young looking woman in her seventies, and Laurent's youngest brother, Thierry. I remember the comfortable quiet, a stalking cat named Ursule, and a three-mile hike through wheat fields, poppies, and roses with the Seine always in view. It was that relaxed quiet that impressed me most—not an isolating, disconcerting stillness but rather the sun and peace of a good Sunday in the country. One breathed in the sense of privacy and family and it felt wonderfully good. If I linger on this episode it is because it so sharply registers on my mind's eye as I reread Babar. This ordered, tight-knit feeling of family is the very essence of Babar. It is too simple to say that my day with the de Brunhoffs helped me to find my Babar bearings, but it is something like the truth.

Jean de Brunhoff, it seems, had to be oblique. Perhaps he knew, instinctively, what I was to learn, that this was the best way to reach and teach children. Beneath the pure fun, the originality of style, and the vivacity of imagination is a serious and touching theme: a father writing to his sons and voicing his natural concern for their welfare, for their lives. At the end of *Babar and His Children*, King Babar says, "Truly it is not easy to bring up a family." And truly it is this hard wisdom that lies at the heart of the books. Why was this such a vital issue in the creation of Babar? In the early 1930s Jean de Brunhoff contracted tuberculosis. Bettina Hürlimann, in her excellent *Three Centuries of Children's Books in Europe*, strongly suggests that had he not been suffering from this disease, there might never have been a Babar. She implies that the books were written by a dying young father, far from his children, as his only means of staying in touch with them. Laurent's memories disagree. He recalls much time spent *en famille*, ". . . winter months in the mountains, summer months in the country, and in between in Paris." He recalls too his father's naturally "humorous and gentle view of people and

My father did many sketches for the cover concept of his first book before arriving at this one, which also incorporates his hand lettering.

Here are some of the designs Jean de Brunhoff created to decorate the children's dining room in the great French transatlantic liner the *Normandie*. They were cut out of wood and mounted on the green walls. For a number of years some of them also decorated the walls of my father's studio in Paris.

things." That Jean had intimations of death must be true. That he was a loving, generous-spirited man is true too. We see it in his work. And, in my many conversations with Laurent, it has been clear that Jean never communicated to his children the private fears and regrets he surely had. He died in 1937. Laurent was twelve at the time and Thierry, the youngest, was not yet three. Jean's bequest to his family, and the world, shines from the books that rushed from his pen at the extraordinary rate of almost one a year between 1931 and 1937. These contain, in Hürlimann's words, "glimpses of things dear to the de Brunhoff family as the background for a father's affectionate counsel"—his counsel on coming of age with grace and kindness, on weathering the inevitable storms of life.

The devotion to family and the circumstances of life that produced Babar must account for the special power and honest sentiment that is the very core of the books. This also helps to explain the balanced emotional climate that is never allowed to go out of control. And here I come back to my first appraisal of Babar, but in a new, most sympathetic light. These books are so traditionally French, filled with what might be considered old-fashioned ideas of manhood, womanhood, and manners. But there is always an underlying emphasis on developing a child's (an elephant child's) personal freedom and individuality through self-control. Not self-control in the repressive sense but defined rather as the awareness of choices of behavior, the awareness that some choices are better than others. "Do you see how in this life one must never be discouraged?" says *la Vieille Dame*. "Let's work hard and cheerfully and we'll continue to be happy." (See page 88.) In *Babar the King* a perfectly wonderful day suddenly turns into a nightmare. Babar is nearly overwhelmed by the arbitrary nature of disaster. But he is comforted by his dream, or vision, of graceful, winged elephants chasing Misfortune away from Celesteville and bringing back Happiness. Then he feels "ever so much better." (See pages 86–87.) He understands that it takes patience, with himself, and perseverance to be happy. It is an earned state of health.

My favorite among Jean's books, *The Travels of Babar*, is full of alarming and very amusing twists of fate. For the one and only time in all the books Babar loses his fine balance and has a good old temper tantrum. He is brought out of it by Celeste. The two alternately comfort each other in times of stress. Here they resolve many crises and, with the good *Vieille Dame* in tow, rush to the mountains "to enjoy the fresh air and try a little skiing." At this point the book stops short so we can study, at leisure, the stupendous double spread of Babar, Celeste, and *la Vieille Dame* calmly gliding down the Swiss slopes. (See pages 54–55.) It is a picture filled with intense concentration, yet soft with the sensuous pleasure of this favorite de Brunhoff sport.

This rooster is a working sketch for my book *Babar's Visit to Bird Island*. Below is a photo of me in my studio in 1949.

After my father died in October 1937, my uncle Michel took charge of finishing the coloring of my father's last two books, *Babar and His Children* and *Babar and Father Christmas*. Both stories had appeared in black and white in 1936 in the British newspaper *The Daily Sketch,* but it was not until after my father's death that they appeared in book form in French. I was just twelve years old, but I knew I would become a painter, and Uncle Michel let me color several pages of the two unfinished books.

After World War Two I became a painter and lived in a studio in Montparnasse. I painted in my own style, but I also wanted to carry on Babar's adventures. My first Babar book, *Babar and That Rascal Arthur,* was published in 1946. For a long time the general public remained unaware of the death of Jean de Brunhoff and thought that the interruption in the Babar series was due to the war. Now I have created many more Babar stories than my father and am older than he ever was, and that is sometimes an eerie feeling.

George Viollon

One of my sketches of Babar as Icarus from *About Air*, published as part of *Babar's Little Library*.

Anne de Brunhoff

This photo was taken in 1980 while I was working on *Babar and the Ghost*. Alone in my studio I shape my books with notes, memory, and imagination . . . and a critical eye that obliges me to constantly revise, rip, and "wastepaper-basket," as, I am sure, my father did. I never want to add permanent characters to the Babar family; however, during the course of a book I often give leading parts to new characters. The Wully-Wully is my idea of a "security blanket," and the crocodiles in *Babar's Mystery* are my conception of perfect villains. In *Babar's Visit to Bird Island* I gave way to a more personal sensibility and to my love of birds. Some people ask me, rather astonished, "Do you only make children's books?" It is true that I enjoy drawing for adults, but I *love* to draw for children. They accept, indeed demand, the greatest freedom in fantasy. Their minds are not limited by preconceptions. They are better able to enjoy wonder, laughter, and tears.

Scale is crucial to de Brunhoff's pictures. Those first editions of Babar have an undiminished splendor with their huge, delectable formats and grand, spacious compositions. They are as pleasing to the eye and as totally original as anything coming out of that fine and rare period of French art. These early editions fell victim to the high cost of production and have been out of print for years. Children, sadly, can no longer "climb into" a Babar book.

No one before, and very few since, has utilized the double-spread illustration to such dazzling, dramatic effect. When Babar and Celeste are taken prisoner, there is a spectacular circus scene. The handsome red arch that denotes the arena floor is also a perfect symbol of their glittering confinement. This is a tour de force of composition and a perfect example of de Brunhoff's sly sense of counterpoint. There is no doubt that the artist is enjoying himself immensely. He has even placed himself in the scene, the young man sitting in the audience pedantically measuring Celeste for a portrait with his outstretched thumb and pencil. (See pages 50–51.) The line of text below the picture is so simple that the art absolutely "blooms" above the words. One can hear Babar's trumpet music. But these books are full of music, both literally and figuratively. The ravishing theatre picture in *Babar the King* (pages 78–79), with every element of architecture fancifully elephantized, is accompanied (at least for me) by the most delicious harpsichord music, Rameau perhaps. And where the grand parade scene from the same book (pages 82–83) is set to a joyous march, Berlioz would be wonderfully suitable. The pictures, by the way, actually move rhythmically in step if you keep your eye on those stolid elephant feet, all thumpingly clumping to the same measure. Color, costume, high comedy mixed with touching solemnity, blend into a characteristic composition that appears ingeniously simple on the surface but is, in fact, extravagantly complex. This is one of my favorite Babar pictures. And it makes a superb psychological point. The celebration catches Babar, and all of Celesteville, at the very peak of happiness and security. Immediately following, and in a series of swift, comic book style squares, shockingly unlike the grandeur of the previous picture, we see the deterioration of that happiness: the near death of *la Vieille Dame* from snakebite. The composition falls apart and only comes together again in the double spread of Babar's vision (pages 86–87) and, not surprisingly, at the very end when we are treated to a small version of that selfsame parade. It is still led by the blithe-spirited Zephir, this time carrying a flag with the motto "Long Live Happiness." (See page 88.)

The little known *Babar and His Children* is the most moving of the series. How happy Babar is to be the father of three little elephants! He knows well how to love his babies. After all, his own brief childhood was graced with the most intense and happy mother's love. And like all wise elephants, Babar does not forget. He never forgets *la Vieille Dame* and he never forgets his mother. "He often stands at the window, thinking sadly of his childhood, and cries when he remembers his mother." Although Babar finds a wonderful second mother in *la Vieille Dame*, this does not erase his early loss. That permeates all the books, but it is never allowed to overwhelm or destroy Babar's self-confidence. It is living that concerns and delights de Brunhoff. He recognizes death as inseparable from the fixed order of things and is never obsessed with it.

At this point I cannot resist quoting Laurent on the death of the old elephant king in *The Story of Babar*. "I do not want to be cynical," he said, "but he dies for the purpose of the plot, to make room for Babar! It is also done in a way to show death as a natural thing." How similar to the death of Babar's mother. How like de Brunhoff's own death, a natural occurrence moving the plot along.

The precious sense of reason that at first struck me as lack of feeling now moves and excites me. Babar "the very good little elephant" deserves his kingdom. He is noble, certainly, and it is by proving this inner worth that he gains his position in life. But de Brunhoff's lessons are suggested in a tone at once so right and humorous, so engaging, that they are irresistible. The grace and graphic charm are almost sufficient by themselves, but to deny the message is to deny the full weight of Jean de Brunhoff's genius. I would like to carry this thought a bit further because it seems to me that Laurent de Brunhoff's Babars are both a continuation of the order his father bequeathed and an answering letter back from son to father. A letter brimming with health and pleasure, confirming all those father's fondest hopes.

Bon anniversaire, Babar, *à votre santé*.

MAURICE SENDAK
New York, April 1981

Anne de Brunhoff

My life with my wife, Marie-Claude (pictured here with me in 1978), and our children Anne, born in 1952, and Antoine, born in 1954, has inspired incidents, settings, ideas for my books. But I have always tried to respect the style and spirit of Babar as created by my father, Jean de Brunhoff.

THE STORY
OF
BABAR

IN THE great forest a little elephant was born. His name was Babar. His mother loved
him very much. She rocked him to sleep with her trunk while singing softly to him.

Babar grew bigger. Soon he played with the other little elephants.

He was a very good little elephant. See him digging in the sand with his shell?

One day, Babar was riding happily on his mother's back when a wicked hunter, hidden behind some bushes, shot at them.

The hunter's shot killed Babar's mother! The monkey hid, the birds flew away, and Babar cried. Then the hunter ran up to catch poor Babar too.

Babar ran away because he was afraid of the hunter. After several days, very tired indeed, he came to a town.

He hardly knew what to make of it because this was the first time that he had seen so many houses. So many things were new to him! The broad streets! The automobiles and buses!

Babar was especially interested in the way the gentlemen looked. He said to himself, "They are very well dressed. I would like to have some fine clothes too!"

Luckily a very rich Old Lady understood that he was longing for a fine suit. She liked to make people happy, so she gave him her purse. Babar said politely, "Thank you, madame."

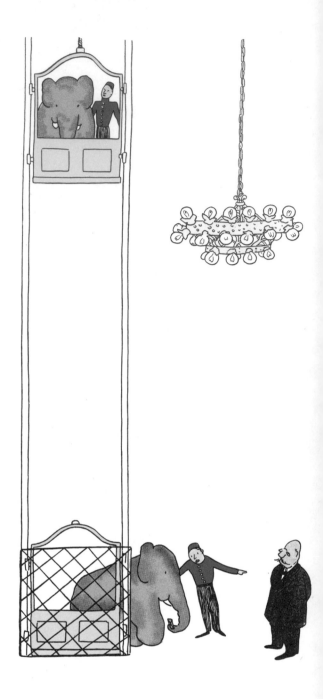

Without wasting time, Babar went into a big store. He took the elevator and had such fun riding up and down, he did not want to stop. But the elevator boy said, "This is not a toy, Mr. Elephant."

Babar then bought himself a shirt
with a collar and tie,

a suit of a becoming shade of green,

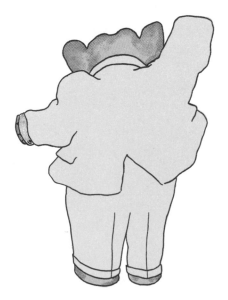

then a handsome derby hat, and also
shoes with spats.

23

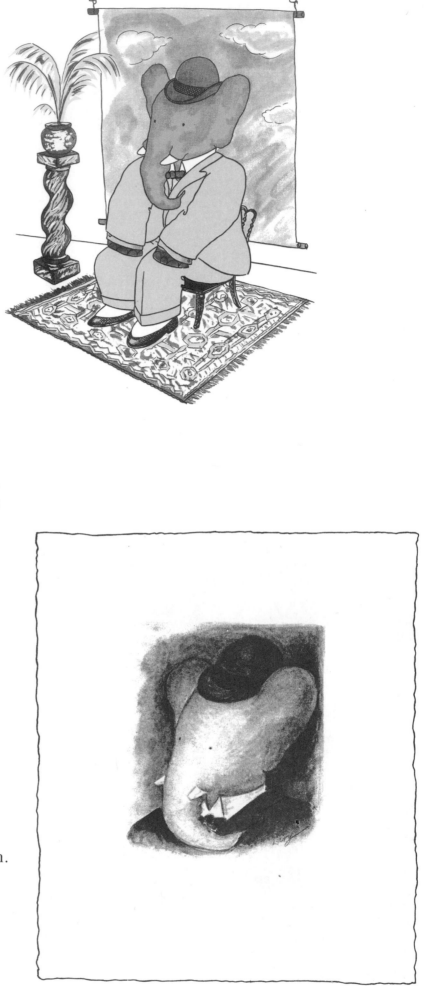

Well satisfied with his purchases and feeling very elegant indeed, Babar went to the photographer to have his picture taken.

And here is his photograph.

Babar dined with his friend, the Old Lady. She thought he looked very smart in his new clothes.

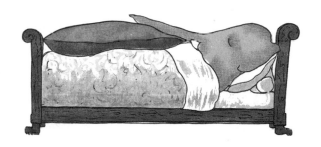

After dinner, because he was tired, he went to bed and fell asleep very quickly.

The Old Lady invited Babar to live in her house. In the mornings he did sitting-up exercises with her,

and then he took his bath.

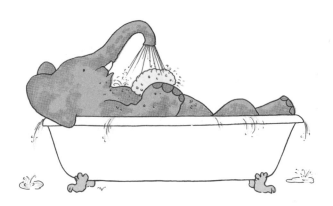

He went out for an automobile ride every day. The Old Lady gave him a car.
She gave Babar whatever he wanted.

A learned professor gave him lessons. Babar paid attention and did well in his work. He was a good pupil and made rapid progress.

In the evening, after dinner, Babar told the Old Lady's friends all about his life in the great forest.

However, Babar was not quite happy, for he missed playing in the great forest with his little cousins and his friends, the monkeys. He often stood at the window, thinking sadly of his childhood, and he cried when he remembered his mother.

Two years passed. One day Babar saw two little elephants coming. They had no clothes on. "It's Arthur and Celeste, my little cousins!" said Babar to the Old Lady.

Babar kissed them affectionately and hurried off to buy them some fine clothes.

Meanwhile, in the forest, the elephants were calling and hunting high and low for Arthur and Celeste. Their mothers were very worried.

Fortunately, in flying over the town, an old marabou bird saw the children. He flew back quickly to tell everyone where they had gone.

The mothers of Arthur and Celeste came to town to fetch them. They were very happy to see that their children were safe, but they scolded them just the same for running away.

Babar made up his mind to go back with Arthur and Celeste and their mothers to see the great forest again. The Old Lady helped him to pack his trunk.

When they were all ready to start, Babar kissed the Old Lady good-bye. He would have been happy to go if it weren't for leaving her. But he promised to come back, for he would never forget her.

And so Babar went away. There was no room in the car for the elephants' mothers, so they ran behind, lifting their trunks to avoid breathing the dust. The Old Lady was left alone. Sadly she wondered, "When shall I see my little Babar again?"

That very day the King of the elephants had eaten a bad mushroom. It poisoned him and he died. This was a great calamity. After the funeral the three oldest elephants held a meeting to choose a new King. Just then they heard a noise. They turned around. Guess what they saw? Babar arriving in his car and all the elephants running and shouting: "Here they are! Here they are! Hello, Babar! Hello, Arthur! Hello, Celeste! What beautiful clothes! What a beautiful car!"

Then Cornelius, the oldest elephant, said, "Why not choose Babar for King? He has learned so much in the city." The other elephants agreed.

"If I am King," said Babar, "Celeste will be your Queen."

Then Babar said, "You have good ideas, Cornelius. I will therefore make you a general, and when I get my crown, I will give you my hat. When I marry Celeste, we will have a splendid party in honor of our marriage."

Then, turning to the birds, Babar asked them to go and invite all the animals to the festivities, and he told the dromedary to go to the town and buy some beautiful wedding clothes.

The very next week, the wedding guests began to arrive. The dromedary returned with Babar's and Celeste's wedding clothes just in time for the ceremony.

After the wedding and the coronation everybody danced merrily.

The festivities ended just as night fell and the stars rose in the sky. King Babar and Queen Celeste were very happy.

Now the world was asleep. The guests had gone home, happy, though tired from too much dancing. They would long remember this great celebration.

THE TRAVELS
OF
BABAR

BABAR, THE YOUNG King of the elephants, and his wife, Queen Celeste, were going on their wedding trip in a balloon. "Good-bye! See you soon!" cried the elephants as they watched the balloon rise and drift away.

Arthur, Babar's little cousin, waved his beret. Old Cornelius, who was chief over all the elephants when the King was away, anxiously sighed, "I do hope they won't have any accidents!"

The country of the elephants was now far away. The balloon glided noiselessly in the sky. Babar and Celeste admired the landscape below. What a beautiful journey! The air was balmy, the wind was gentle. There was the ocean, the big blue ocean.

Suddenly the balloon was blown out to sea by a violent storm. Babar and Celeste trembled with fear and clung to the basket.

By extraordinary good fortune, just as the balloon was about to fall into the sea, a final puff of wind blew it to an island, where it flattened out and collapsed.

"You aren't hurt, Celeste, are you?" Babar inquired anxiously. "No! Well then, look, we are saved!"

Leaving the wrecked balloon on the beach, Babar and Celeste picked up their belongings and went off to seek shelter.

Celeste hung up their clothes to dry while Babar lighted a fire and began preparing breakfast.

Babar and Celeste settled themselves comfortably. They set up their tent. Then they sat on some large stones and ate an excellent rice broth well-sweetened and cooked to perfection. "We are not so badly off," said Babar.

After breakfast Babar and Celeste rested on the seashore. Suddenly a whale came to the surface and spouted. Babar said, "Good morning, Mrs. Whale. I am Babar and here is my wife, Celeste. We have had a balloon accident. Can you help us to get away from here?"

"I will be very happy to help you," said the whale. "Quick, get on my back and hold tight so you don't slip off. Are you ready? Get set. Let's go!"

A few days later Babar and Celeste were resting on a reef. Just then a school of little fish swam by.

"I am going to eat up some of these," said the whale. "I'll be back in a minute." But she did not come back. She forgot!

After hours spent on their little reef, without even a drop of fresh water, they finally spied a ship passing quite near them. It was a big steamer with three funnels.

Babar and Celeste called out and yelled as loudly as they could, but no one heard them. They tried signaling with their trunks and with their arms. Would they ever attract someonc's attention?

Finally somebody saw them! A lifeboat rescued Babar and Celeste while the excited passengers all watched.

A week later the huge ship steamed slowly into a big harbor. All the passengers went down the gangplank. Babar and Celeste were not allowed to go. They had lost their crowns, so no one believed they were King and Queen of the elephants.

The Captain of the ship ordered them locked up in the ship's stables. "They give us straw to sleep on!" cried Babar angrily.

The Captain came in with an animal trainer, Fernando. "You can have these elephants for your circus," he said. Fernando led away his two pupils.

"Be patient, Babar," whispered Celeste. "We will get home somehow and see Cornelius and Arthur."

Fernando took Babar and Celeste to his circus.

He made Babar play a trumpet while Celeste danced! They were very unhappy.

One day the circus came to the town where Babar had met his friend the Old Lady. So, at night, while Fernando was in bed, Babar and Celeste escaped and went to find her. He had never forgotten her.

Babar found the house easily and rang the bell. The Old Lady put on her wrapper, stepped out onto her balcony, and called, "Who's there?"

"Babar and Celeste," they answered her.

The Old Lady was overjoyed. Babar and Celeste were happy too, for they would never have to go back to the circus. Soon they would rejoin Arthur and Cornelius. The Old Lady promised to help them.

At the circus their escape was soon discovered.

"Stop! Thief! My elephants have been stolen!" cried the excited Fernando.

"Little ones, oh little ones, where are you hiding?" the clowns called.

But Babar and Celeste would not be caught again. They were on their way to the station with the Old Lady. They needed a few days' rest before returning to their own land.

The three of them went to the mountains to enjoy the fresh air and try a little skiing.

Then they left by plane to return home. Babar was anxious to show the Old Lady his beautiful country. But when they got there, nothing was left of the great forest. There were no flowers, no birds. Everyone was sad.

"Alas," said Cornelius. "The rhinoceroses have declared war on us."
Celeste and the Old Lady took care of the wounded elephants and Babar
went off to join the elephant army.

57

At the camp of the rhinoceroses the soldiers were awaiting orders. "We will once again defeat the elephants," they thought. "Then the war will be over and we can all go home."

Spiteful old Rataxes maliciously said to his friend, General Pamir: "Hah! Hah! Hah! Pretty soon we will tweak the ears of this young King Babar and punish that rascal Arthur."

At the camp of the elephants Babar brought his army new courage. He disguised his biggest soldiers, painting their tails bright red, and near their tails on either side he painted large, frightening eyes.

Arthur set to work making wigs. He worked as hard as he could so he would be forgiven. The war was really Arthur's fault. It had started when that rascal Arthur had tied a big firecracker to Rataxes's tail.

On the day of the battle, at just the right moment, the disguised
elephants came out of hiding. Babar's bright idea succeeded!

The rhinoceroses thought they were monsters and, terrified, they retreated in great disorder. King Babar was a mighty fine general.

The rhinoceroses fled and kept running! Pamir and Rataxes were taken prisoner and hung their heads in shame. What a glorious day for the elephants! In chorus they all cried:

"Bravo, Babar, bravo! Victory! Victory! The war is over! How perfectly splendid!"

The next day, before all of the elephants, Babar and Celeste put on their royal garments and their new crowns and rewarded the Old Lady, who had been so good to them and had cared for the wounded. They gave her eleven singing canaries and a cunning little monkey.

After the ceremony Babar, Celeste, and the Old Lady sat and chatted under the palm trees. "And what are we going to do next?" asked the Old Lady.

"I am going to try to rule my kingdom wisely," answered Babar, "and if you will remain with us, you can help me make my subjects happy."

BABAR
THE KING

O FF IN THE country of the elephants King Babar and Queen Celeste
were rejoicing. They had signed a treaty of peace with the rhinoceros, and their
friend, the Old Lady, had consented to remain with them. She often told the
children stories. Her little monkey, Zephir, perched in a tree, would listen too.

Leaving the Old Lady with Queen Celeste, Babar went for a walk along the banks of a large lake with Cornelius, the oldest and wisest of all the elephants, and said to him, "This countryside is so beautiful that I would like to see it every day as I wake up.

"We must build our city here. Our houses shall be
on the shores of the lake and shall be surrounded
with flowers and birds." Zephir, who had followed
them, wanted to catch a butterfly that he saw.

While chasing the butterfly, Zephir met his friend, Arthur, the young cousin of the King and Queen, who was hunting for snails. All of a sudden they saw more dromedaries than they could count.

The dromedaries were bringing Babar the things he had bought on his honeymoon. Babar thanked them. "You must be tired, gentlemen. Won't you rest under the shade of the palm trees?" Then, turning to the Old Lady and Cornelius, he said, "Now we will be able to build our city."

Babar stood on a packing case and proclaimed: "I have in these trunks gifts for all of you. I will give them out after we build our city. I suggest we name our city of elephants Celesteville, in honor of our Queen."

The elephants set to work. They cut down trees, moved stones, sawed wood, and dug holes. The Old Lady played the phonograph for them, and Babar played the trumpet. The elephants opened their ears wide to hear.

All the birds gathered to discuss what the elephants were up to. The pelicans and the flamingos twittered and chirped. The parrots kept repeating, "Come and see Celesteville, the most beautiful of all cities!"

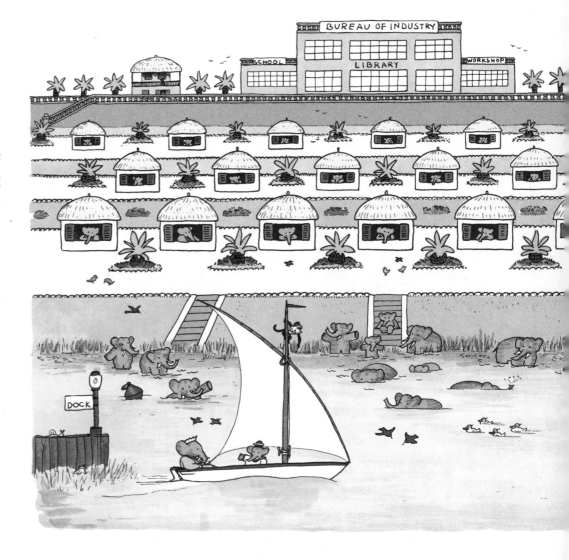

Here is Celesteville! The elephants just finished building it. Babar went for a sail with Arthur and Zephir. He was well satisfied with his new capital. Each elephant had his own house. The big lake was visible from all their windows. The Bureau of Industry was next door to the Amusement Hall, which was very practical and convenient.

Then Babar kept his promise. He gave a gift to each elephant and also sturdy clothes for workdays and rich, beautiful clothes for holidays. After thanking their King most heartily, the elephants all went home dancing with glee.

Babar decided that the next Sunday all the elephants would dress in their best clothes and assemble in the gardens of the Amusement Park. The gardeners had much to do. They raked the paths, watered the flower beds, and set out the last flowerpots.

The elephant children planned a surprise for Babar and Celeste. They asked Cornelius to teach them the song of the elephants. Arthur had the idea. They were very attentive, kept time, and learned it perfectly by Sunday.

72

The cooks prepared cakes and dainties of all kinds. Queen Celeste came to help them. Zephir came, too, with Arthur. He tasted the vanilla cream to see if it was just right. First he put in his finger, then his hand, and then his arm. In order to have one last taste Zephir bent his head, stuck out his tongue, and *plouf!*—in he fell head first.

At this sound the chief cook looked around and, greatly annoyed, fished Zephir out by the tail. The soup chef burst out laughing. Arthur hid. Poor little Zephir was a sight, all yellow and sticky. Celeste scolded him and cleaned him up.

Sunday came at last. In the gardens of the Amusement Park the elephants sauntered about dressed magnificently. The children sung their song, and Babar kissed each one of them.

The cakes were delicious! What a wonderful day! Unfortunately it was over all too soon. The Old Lady was already organizing the last round of hide-and-seek.

The next day, after their morning dip in the lake, the children went to school. They were glad to find their dear teacher, the Old Lady, waiting for them. Lessons were never tiresome when she taught.

After settling the little ones at their tasks, she turned her attention to the older ones and asked them: "Two times two?" "Three," answered Arthur. "No, no, four," said his neighbor, Ottilie. "Four," repeated Arthur. "I'll not forget that again, teacher."

Tapitor

Capoulosse Fandago

Barbacol

Podular

Pilophage Justinen

Doulamor

Poutifour

Hatchibombotar Olur

Coco

All the elephants who were too old to attend classes chose a trade. There was a cobbler, a tailor, a sculptor, a painter, a musician, a farmer, a street cleaner, and an auto repairman. There was even a clown to keep them all laughing and gay.

At Celesteville all the elephants worked in the morning, and in the afternoon they could do as they pleased. They played, went for walks, read, and dreamed. Babar and Celeste liked to play tennis with Mr. and Mrs. Pilophage.

The children played with Coco, the clown. They also had a shallow pool for sailing their boats, and many other games besides.

But what the elephants liked best of all was the theatre.

Babar and Celeste visited the Old Lady and were amazed to hear Arthur and Zephir play the cello and violin. "It is wonderful!" said Celeste, and Babar added, "My dear children, I am pleased with you."

Babar told them to go to the pastry shop and select as many cakes as they liked. Arthur and Zephir were very happy, but they were even more delighted when, on Prize Day, Cornelius read out: "First prize for music: a tie between Arthur and Zephir." Very proudly, with wreaths on their heads, they went back to their seats. Cornelius made a noble speech.

"And now I wish you all a pleasant holiday!" he ended up. Everyone applauded loudly. Then, quite weary, Cornelius sat down, but alas and alack, his fine hat was on the chair, and he crushed it completely.

"A regular pancake!" said Zephir. Cornelius was aghast and sadly looked at what was left of his hat. What would he wear on the next formal occasion? The Old Lady promised to sew some plumes on Cornelius's old derby.

A big celebration was planned on the anniversary of the founding of Celesteville. The weather was perfect. Arthur marched at the head of the parade with Zephir and the band. Cornelius followed, his hat completely transformed. Then came the soldiers and the trade companies. All those who were not marching watched this unforgettable spectacle.

On his way home from the celebration Zephir noticed a curious stick. Horrors! It was a snake, which reared up and cruelly bit the Old Lady. Arthur furiously smashed his bugle on the snake and killed it.

The Old Lady's arm swelled, and she hastened to the hospital. Dr.
Capoulosse took care of her and gave her a hypodermic of serum. Zephir
remained with his mistress. Dr. Capoulosse told Babar that she was ill.

When Babar left the hospital, he heard cries of "Fire! Fire!" Cornelius's house was on fire. The stairway was already full of smoke. The firemen succeeded in rescuing Cornelius, but he was half suffocated and a burning beam had injured him.

Dr. Capoulosse gave Cornelius first aid before having him moved to the hospital. A match that Cornelius thought he had thrown into the ashtray had fallen, still lighted, into the trash basket and had started this terrible fire.

That night, when Babar went to bed, he shut his eyes but could not sleep. "What a dreadful day!" he thought. "It began so well. Why did it have to end so badly? Before these two accidents we were all so happy and peaceful at Celesteville! We had forgotten that misfortune existed! Oh, my dear old Cornelius, and you, dear Old Lady, I would give my crown to see you cured. Capoulosse was to telephone me any news. Oh! How long this night seems, and how worried I am!"

Babar finally dropped off to sleep, but his sleep was restless and soon *he dreamed:* He heard a knocking on his door. Tap! Tap! Then a voice said: "It is I, Misfortune, with some of my companions, come to pay you a visit." Babar looked out the window and saw a frightful old woman surrounded by flabby, ugly beasts. He opened his mouth to shout: "Ugh! Faugh! Go away quickly." But he stopped to listen to a faint noise—*frr! frr! frr!*—as of birds flying in a flock, and he saw coming toward him . . .

. . . graceful winged elephants who chased Misfortune away from Celesteville and brought back Happiness. At this point he awoke and felt ever so much better.

Babar dressed and ran to the hospital. Oh joy! His two patients were walking in the garden. "We are all well again," said Cornelius.

A week later the Old Lady said to her two friends: "Do you see how in this life one must never be discouraged? The vicious snake didn't kill me, and Cornelius is completely recovered. Let's work hard and cheerfully and we'll continue to be happy."

And since then, everyone in elephant country has been happy and contented.

BABAR'S
BIRTHDAY SURPRISE

ONE DAY Podular, the sculptor, was putting the finishing touches on a pretty little statue of his friend, King Babar. Zephir, the monkey, watched.

Queen Celeste entered Podular's studio with the Old Lady and Cousin Arthur. They all admired Podular's work.

When the statue was finished, Celeste spoke to Podular privately. "I would like to surprise Babar for his birthday," she said. "Would you carve a giant statue of him in the side of the mountain?"

Podular was enthusiastic. "But Babar must suspect nothing," warned Celeste.

Aided by Zephir, Podular loaded his truck. Without losing a minute, they left for the mountain. Finally they found a place where the stone seemed well suited for carving. They cut down some trees and raised a scaffold against the mountainside. Now Podular was ready to start his biggest and most important sculpture ever!

Cesarine, the giraffe, was very excited. Suddenly a car horn tooted.

"Look out!" cried the giraffe. "It might be Babar!"

"It's all right, Cesarine," said the sculptor calmly. He recognized the horn of Arthur's red car and climbed down the scaffold to greet Arthur.

The head of the statue was completely finished. Podular worked hard
on Babar's necktie. "At least the most
difficult part is done," he thought.

Suddenly the marabous began to cry
out, "Someone is coming here on a
bicycle!"

Arthur held his breath.

"All is lost," sighed Podular.

But no. It was not Babar on his bicycle. It was three bicycles. Babar's children had come to see the statue.

"Hi, Alexander! Pom! Flora!" Podular cried to them. "It is nice of you to come see us."

"Oh! How handsome Papa is as a mountain!" said Alexander.

In the palace kitchens the Old Lady and Celeste came to see the cooks. No doubt about it—the cakes would be delicious!

Babar and Celeste took a walk together.

Celeste was nervous because Babar was so deep in thought. "Does he suspect something?" she wondered.

But Babar told her that he was upset about losing his pipe the other day. Celeste promised herself that she would give him a beautiful new pipe.

Back in Celesteville everyone was busy. Babar's birthday was to be a wonderful celebration.

On the top of the mountain, behind the head of the statue, Podular and his friends were enjoying a picnic. They could see the city, the palace, and the river off in the distance. But who was coming up the road by bicycle?

It was Babar! This time it really was! Catastrophe! Would the birthday secret be discovered at the last moment?

Flora and Alexander were very worried as they watched from below, hidden in the underbrush.

"Hello, Babar," said Cesarine.

"I am looking for my pipe," Babar said to the giraffe. "I wonder if it fell around here."

"I was just playing with it," said a marabou. "Now, where did I leave it?"

At that very moment Flora stepped on the pipe. Snap! It broke into two pieces.

Hearing the noise, Babar turned around. "What was that?" he asked.

"I am afraid I just stepped on your pipe," one of the marabous answered quickly.

Immediately the two birds brought Babar the pieces of his pipe while Flora and Alexander tried to make themselves small behind the bushes.

"I really love this pipe," said Babar. "I will glue it together again."

"Saved! Babar did not see the statue," cried the children. In their joy, they jumped wildly about on the scaffolding.

"Stop that!" scolded Podular. Too late. The whole scaffolding collapsed.

What a fall! "Arthur has hurt his trunk," said the sculptor.

Zephir drove off and returned with Dr. Capoulosse, who rolled a long bandage around Arthur's trunk.

The following day a crowd of elephants headed toward the mountain. Babar was very happy. "How nice of you, Celeste, to organize this celebration! I love to lunch on the grass."

Celeste smiled. She was thinking that soon Babar would be even happier. And the Old Lady had a mysterious smile on her face too.

As they drew near, Babar saw millions of birds covering the mountainside. He found the spectacle very beautiful. Astonished, he asked, "Are they part of the festival?"

"Of course," Celeste answered. "Everybody wanted to come. For, as you will see, there is a surprise."

"Oh yes, a surprise," repeated Cornelius as he trotted away.

Cornelius assembled the musicians of the Royal Guard. The trumpets sounded the fanfare. At a signal all the birds covering the mountain flew up at the same time. The air was filled with the loud fluttering of wings.

Babar was stupefied. "Why, it's me! Extraordinary!" he said, hugging Celeste. "What a splendid statue. Podular, my friend, I congratulate you. Dear Celeste, I am very moved. What an enormous surprise!"

After lunch the cooks from the palace brought a wonderful cake.

"Happy birthday!" shouted the children.

Then Cornelius said, "Babar, it is up to you to cut the cake."

"Oh yes, quickly," added Arthur, sounding funny because of the bandages on his trunk.

Everyone cried, "Happy Birthday!"

Except for the weary Podular, who was fast asleep.

BABAR'S
MYSTERY

PEOPLE CAME from all over the world to Celesteville-on-the-Sea. It had the most beautiful beach in the land of the elephants. King Babar and his family spent all their vacations there.

They stayed at the Grand Hotel with their children, Pom, Flora, and Alexander. They all enjoyed strolling on the promenade that ran along the shore.

"Wait for us," Arthur and the Old Lady shouted from the terrace of the hotel.

The sun was very strong, so big umbrellas lined the beach. Some bathers played, some relaxed, and some went into the water. The Old Lady thought there were too many people. "I adore this place, but there is too much noise," she said with a sigh. "I need quiet and solitude to write my book."

"It's very simple," Celeste told her. "You can work in the lighthouse. There you will hear nothing but the splash of waves and the cries of gulls." The Old Lady was delighted by the idea, and she settled in at once with her cat and her typewriter. Arthur arrived ahead of them all—on his motorbike.

When Babar, Celeste, and Arthur went back to the hotel, they were greeted by shouts from the children. "The piano has been stolen. Some furniture movers said they were going to bring another one for the concert. But they left in a truck and never came back. Nobody guessed they were thieves!"

Flora showed everybody the glove she had found on the sidewalk. "If we can find the owner of the other glove, we will have the thief."

"A valuable clue," cried Arthur. "I will start an investigation at once."

The Old Lady did not plan to come back for lunch. So Babar and Celeste went to the market to buy food for her picnic lunch.

Arthur questioned a glove merchant. "Madame, have you recently sold a pair of gloves like this one? It is the glove of a thief, we think."

"No, young man, I don't sell this brand. But I think my friend Patamousse at Mont Saint Georges has some like it. He will be glad to help you."

The Old Lady had asked that absolutely no one bother her while she was writing her memoirs. So Babar sent the lunch up in a basket by using a rope and pulley.

Arthur appeared on his motorbike to tell the results of his inquiry.

"Well, well," Babar decided. "We will all go to Mont Saint Georges."

Babar drove the family in his shiny red car. Arthur preferred to go on his motorbike.

"You know," said Alexander, "at high tide Mont Saint Georges is surrounded by water. You must go by boat."

Babar parked the car and walked toward the castle ramparts with Celeste, Pom, Flora, and Alexander. Arthur made sure his motorbike was standing securely. What a crowd! The tourists were coming to Mont Saint Georges in busloads.

"Our friend the Old Lady was wise not to come," said Celeste with a laugh. "She would have detested all the hubbub."

"But it is so beautiful," said Babar, "that we must not forget to take back some postcards for her."

The narrow streets were full of sight-seers. Babar, Celeste, and the children strolled around, looking at all the souvenir and antique shops. Finally Arthur located the shop of Patamousse, the glove merchant. "Sir, have you sold a pair of gloves like this?" he asked the hippopotamus.

Unfortunately the merchant had sold many such gloves, so he could not give Arthur any very precise information. "But," he said, "I seem to recall that the last customer to buy a pair like that was a lion."

"Ah," said Arthur, "perhaps he is my thief."

At last it was time to leave, and all of them walked away from the castle ramparts—only to find that their car had disappeared! "Where is my car?" cried Babar. "Someone has stolen my brand-new car!" Babar was in a state. He went around asking all the bus drivers if they had seen his red car.

One of them remembered seeing such a car being driven by a crocodile.

"No, you are wrong," said another. "It was a lion."

A third driver claimed to have seen an elephant at the wheel.

"Which one am I to believe?" Babar wondered helplessly. "Come, we will have to go back by bus."

Back at the hotel Babar told his family, "A new statue is being unveiled at the Celesteville Seashore Theatre, and I must give a speech. I want you to keep your eyes open for the thief."

Pom, Flora, and Alexander ran to the theatre, looking for the thief. Outside, decorators were hanging up beautiful flowers. One of them, a lion, wore a glove like the one Flora had found. Was he the thief? But then they saw that the lion was wearing gloves on both hands. He did not lose a glove, so he could not be the thief.

Later Babar was finishing his speech in front of the statue, which was covered with a sheet. Arthur watched the crowd of spectators, hoping that some new clue would put him on the trail of the thieves. Finally Babar said, "And I wish much joy to all the future audiences at the Celesteville Seashore Theatre." Then, raising his trunk, he prepared to uncover the statue. Everyone held his breath. At last they would see the famous gold statue!

Babar gave a sharp tug at the sheet;
the cloth slid off. . . . NO STATUE!
. . . Someone had stolen it! In its place
there was a crude dummy made from a
barrel and some pieces of wood.

"Catch those thieves!"

"We must catch those thieves!"
shouted the crowd. "There must be a
whole gang of them." "First the piano,
then Babar's car, and now the statue!"
"This is too much. We have got to catch
the scoundrels."

Arthur jumped on his motorbike and drove onto the main road. He spied a red car speeding away. Babar's car! On the back seat there was a big, peculiar-looking bundle. "I have found the thieves at last!" But he suddenly lost their trail at a street corner. Since he was near the lighthouse, he stopped to see the Old Lady. He asked her if she had heard a car go past.

"Yes, I did hear a car just now," she said. "It must have stopped very near here." She and Arthur snuck up to a little shed. Arthur put a large box under the window and peeked inside. What did he see?

Four crocodiles dancing with joy around the unwrapped statue! Babar's car was there, and the piano too. One of the thieves was wearing the glove! He sneered, "Ha! Ha! I would have liked to see Babar's face when he discovered the barrel and the pieces of wood."

"Hurry up," said another thief. "We must go to our meeting at the harbor at once."

Arthur followed them to the harbor and spied on their meeting with a nasty-looking rhinoceros. Then he rowed away quietly and found Babar. Together they prepared a plan.

That night the crocodiles began to put their loot on a big boat. They thought they were very clever. Suddenly, at a sign from Babar, the Old Lady shouted, "Stop, thieves!"

"Aha! Old Lady!" shouted the crocodiles. "You are not going to have a chance to tell Babar about our business. We will take you away with us on the boat." The crocodiles, who were not very smart, rushed into the lighthouse.

The minute they were inside, Babar slammed the door. Without a moment's hesitation the Old Lady and her cat got into the basket and Arthur lowered her to the ground. Now the crocodiles were prisoners in the lighthouse! How they moaned about their bad luck!

The next day everyone read the newspaper account.

ROBBERS CAUGHT!

Discovered by Arthur and the Old Lady, the robbers — a gang of four crocodiles — have been arrested thanks to King Babar's bold strategy. The courage of our dear Old Lady has won everyone's admiration. The leader of the gang, a rhinoceros, intended to sell the statue and leave on a trip in Babar's car. The Coast Guard caught him. As for the theft of the piano, it seemed to have been the idea of the crocodiles, who call themselves musicians. . . .

BABAR
AND THE
WULLY-WULLY

ONE MORNING Pom, Flora, and Alexander took a stroll.
Suddenly they came upon a strange little animal.

"That is a Wully-Wully," said Pom. "An animal that is
seldom seen."

"Let's take him home," said Alexander.

In the gardens of Celesteville Babar said, "Yes, this is certainly a Wully-Wully. He is very gentle-looking and quite lovable."

The Old Lady smiled fondly at the small creature.

128

The Wully-Wully had a very good time in Babar's house. The toys of Pom, Flora, and Alexander fascinated him, especially the electric train. He watched it go around him hour after hour.

The Wully-Wully ate with the rest of the family, but instead of sitting down with them, he preferred to hang upside down by his tail. He also slept in that position—like a bat.

The Wully-Wully liked the country too, so the children took him on a picnic. While they were unpacking the food, Rataxes, the rhinoceros, spied on them.

"A Wully-Wully!" he said. "If I can snatch him away, he'll be mine."

The little pet suspected nothing, and neither did the children.

Suddenly Rataxes jumped out from behind the bush, shoved the little elephants out of the way, and seized the Wully-Wully, who let out a piercing cry. But what could he do against a huge rhinoceros?

Rataxes jumped into his car with the Wully-Wully and drove off, laughing. Arthur and the others chased after him, but the thief got away. They were in despair. They thought they had lost their Wully-Wully forever.

They rushed back to the garden to find Zephir.

"You must help us," said Pom.

After he had heard the whole story, the little monkey said, "Arthur, let's go on a search."

The two scouts crept up to the city of the rhinos. Zephir looked through his binoculars.

He could see the little Wully-Wully tied by a leash. Rataxes didn't let him loose for an instant.

To get closer to the city of the rhinos without being seen, Arthur put on one of his disguises. Dressed like a camel, he walked behind the bushes. Zephir looked like someone out for a camel ride.

They could see that Wully-Wully looked very unhappy. "How can we save him?" Arthur asked.

"Just you wait, Rataxes," threatened Zephir. "I am going to think up a trick to get into your city."

Later that day a strange hat merchant came to the city of the rhinos. Everybody went to him, for the rhinos adored hats.

Suddenly Rataxes cried, "Arthur, I recognize you. It's off to prison with you!"

Back in Celesteville everybody was worried. Cornelius played cards, but he could not hide his concern. "You never know what that Rataxes will do," he said. The Old Lady agreed.

Babar tried to reassure them. "You just wait," he said. "Arthur and Zephir will be successful. Don't worry."

The children went to bed. But Flora could not sleep. She was too sad.

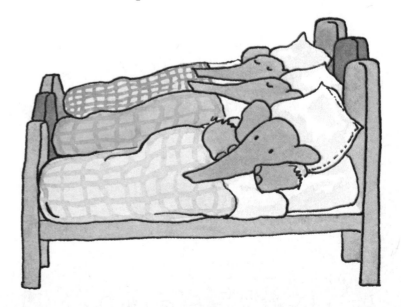

All this time Arthur had been shut up in a tiny, dark cell. Fortunately Rataxes did not catch Zephir. The clever monkey managed to get away and was hiding nearby. As soon as darkness fell, he ran up to the prison and shouted:

"Arthur! I am going to save you! Have courage!"

The guards, outraged by this impudence, chased after him.

It was easy for Zephir to lead the clumsy rhinos away from the prison. They puffed along behind him, shouting, "Beware, you monkey! We'll fix you."

Suddenly, without knowing how it happened, the guards lost all trace of Zephir. Where had he gone? They could not believe it!

After leading the guards astray, Zephir quickly went back to the prison. He got the door open. Arthur was free!

While Arthur hid in the woods, Zephir ran to the palace. "I am going to set the Wully-Wully free," he said, "before someone gives the alarm."

Quietly as a cat Zephir crept inside Rataxes's palace. Arthur watched him vanish right under the noses of the sleeping guards.

Zephir found Rataxes's bedroom without any trouble. The big rhino was sleeping like a log under his heavy quilt.

Wully-Wully was next to the bed. He wagged his tail, for he recognized the little monkey.

"Shhh!" Zephir warned. He took the Wully-Wully in his arms and stole away.

Very early in the morning Babar and Celeste heard shouts under their windows. Everybody rushed out to greet the returning heroes, who were proud of their escapade.

The news spread fast through Celesteville. The elephants all congratulated Arthur and Zephir. They carried them in triumph through the streets.

"Bravo, Arthur! Bravo, Zephir!" they shouted. "You have outwitted Rataxes! Bravo! Long live the Wully-Wully."

Suddenly they all heard a frightful rumbling like an earthquake!

It was Rataxes and his rhinos, sweeping through Celesteville like a hurricane. The elephants were so stunned by this terrible charge that they could not even resist.

The rhinos disappeared in a cloud of

dust, carrying Wully-Wully away with them. The elephants were furious. They shouted, "Down with Rataxes! We want to fight!"

Babar did not want to go to war, but what could he do?

Little Flora was worried. She started thinking: "If there is a war with the rhinos, what will happen to Wully? He could be killed." So without telling anyone, she ran to the city of the rhinos.

When the guards brought the spunky little elephant to Rataxes, the fierce old rhinoceros scowled and said, "Why have you come? Aren't you afraid?"

"Why should I be?" asked Flora.

"Well, you know that Arthur and Zephir played a trick on me," said Rataxes.

Flora did not answer. Instead she asked, "Why do you keep Wully-Wully in a cage? And why did you steal him? He is not yours."

"He is not yours either!" grumbled Rataxes.

"You are right," said Flora. "But I am the one who found him and I never tied him up. I didn't put him in a cage either, yet he stayed with me."

Perplexed, Rataxes scratched his ear. "If I let him out he will run away."

"Perhaps," said Flora. "But he will come back when he wants to." Still troubled, Rataxes agreed to open the cage.

Now the Wully-Wully could go where he wished. Each day he stopped to see Flora and the elephants, but he also visited the city of the rhinos. When Wully-Wully was at Celesteville, Rataxes was likely to be there too, help-ing Flora make a rope swing for the little pet.

Babar watched them and thought, "It's really amazing. Our little Flora has completely tamed the great, rough Rataxes!"

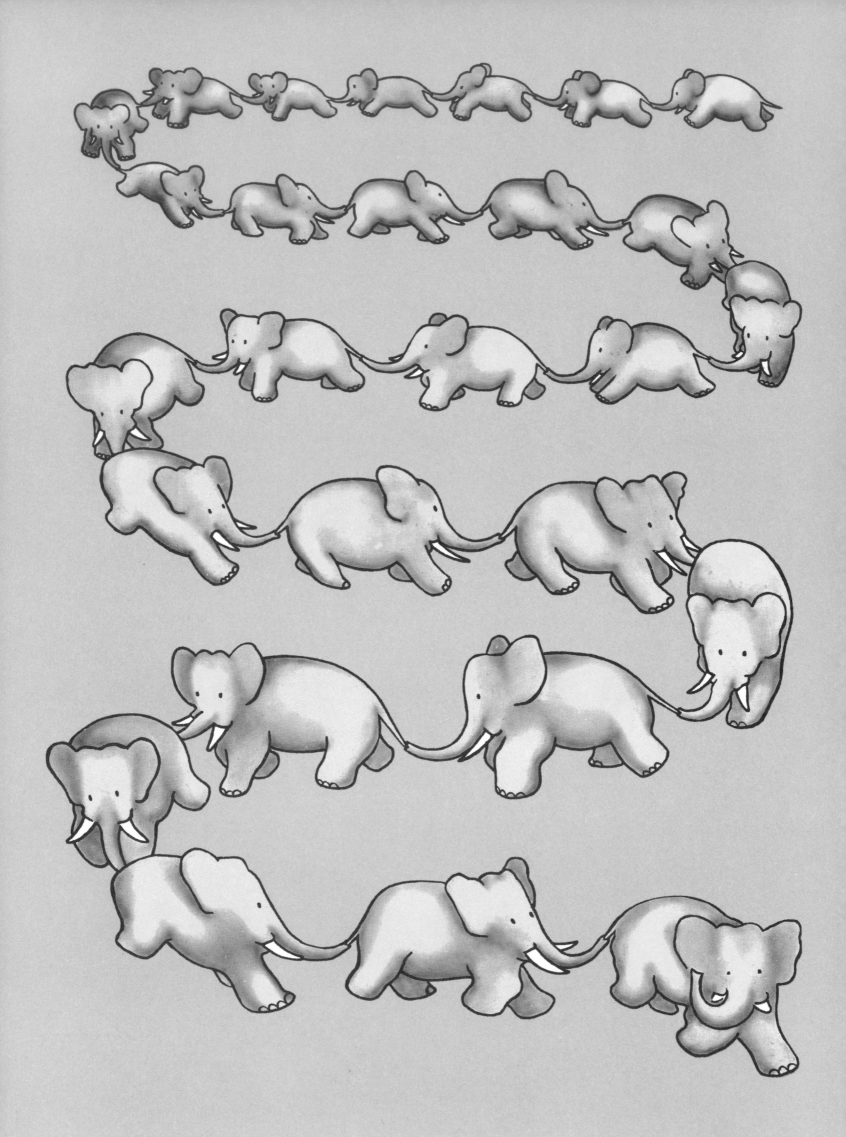